About the Author

Sue Ellis has been working in the world of education for over thirty years, formerly as a secondary school teacher, followed by a Behaviour and Attendance adviser and now a visiting lecturer. She has a wide experience of listening to children's views and frustrations from the pupils she has taught, and bringing up her own two children.

Sue has written these stories for children to enjoy reading about quirky, sassy birds making their way in life through good times and bad, making positive decisions. Sue hopes that her readers will then discuss their feelings about the stories and learn, in turn, to make positive decisions in their own lives.

Sue was born in Liverpool and spent her early years in Crosby. She has lived in York with her husband and family for over thirty years.

SUE ELLIS

PROUD PATRICK PEACOCK AND OTHER STORIES

AUSTIN MACAULEY PUBLISHERS™
LONDON • CAMBRIDGE • NEW YORK • SHARJAH

A CIP catalogue record for this title is available from the British Library.

ISBN 9781787104020 (Paperback)
ISBN 9781787104037 (E-Book)
www.austinmacauley.com

First Published (2017)
Austin Macauley Publishers ™ Ltd
25 Canada Square
Canary Wharf
London
E14 5LQ

Dedication

These stories are dedicated to:

- My trusty band of primary-aged critics whose insight and wisdom never fail to amaze me: Maddy Barker, Amelie Oldfield, Amelie McNiven, Quinn Scott, April and Albert Snow, and Mimi and Giacomo Killough.

- All the inspirational teachers I have been taught by and/or worked with over the years particularly Bernie Cullen from Great Crosby RC Primary School, Sister Siobhan from Seafield Grammar School, John Tomsett former Headteacher at Lady Lumley's School and the Behaviour Team at North Yorkshire Local Authority, (particularly Kerry Chapman from the Enhanced Mainstream School at Barwic Parade Primary who requested a story on 'Telling the Truth').

- David, my wonderful husband, Katie and Robert, my amazing children, and Anita and Geoff Farrell my inspirational parents who always ensure my resilience, self-confidence and self-esteem are intact when the going gets tough. I am blessed!

CONTENTS

Proud Patrick Peacock Eats Humble Pie!

It was a sunny day in June. Cyril Squirrel was out on his first walk of the morning in the Museum Gardens. The Gardens are situated near the River Ouse in the centre of the historic city of York. "Good morning Patrick Peacock," he shouted as Patrick strutted past him, "You are looking very handsome today!"

"I always look handsome!" crowed Patrick, arrogantly puffing out his iridescent blue and green chest. He held his proud head high just like one of the statues inside the Museum, and the crest on his head stood upright like a king's crown. His long tail dragged on the ground behind him. "Another day strutting around my gardens showing off my party of peahens and chicks to my adoring public!" he added.

"The Museum Gardens aren't yours Patrick. They belong to all of us: squirrels, birds, flowers, trees and all the people who enjoy the gardens throughout the year," informed Cyril Squirrel, "Pride comes before a fall Patrick—it's not all about you."

"I am the main attraction here," Patrick retorted with his beak in the air, "I rule the roost in this neck of the woods."

"The people come to enjoy the gardens, visit the Yorkshire Museum and see the historic buildings in the grounds,

Patrick," Cyril replied very patiently, "If you weren't here, they would still come and visit."

"Ah, yes," replied Patrick quickly, "but when I open my tail into its breathtaking fan, everybody stops and stares. Just watch—it's like magic!" Immediately, he stopped on the path by the monkey puzzle tree and spread out his tail feathers. The crowd started to gather round admiring the vibrant colours of blue, green, gold and red and marvelled at the wonderful eyespots at the end of all the feathers. Patrick made all the feathers quiver in the early morning sunshine, and he suddenly became the focus of all the tourists' photographs. He listened to all the people exclaiming how beautiful, gorgeous and magnificent he was and he nodded in agreement. When he finally closed his tail feathers, he was pleased to hear all the sighs of disappointment from the crowd. Patrick moved off up the path to walk across the lawns in front of the museum. The crowd followed him. He knew where the best photographs could be taken of him in order to display his very best features. He walked in front of a bank of splendid white Yorkshire roses. Again he opened his tail feathers so that his dazzling plumage could be seen against the backdrop of white petals. The people sighed at his beauty and Patrick continued to bask in the enjoyment of their admiration. Cyril Squirrel watched from a distance. "It must be just like being a superstar," he thought to himself and scampered off towards the Observatory to find his breakfast.

Later on that day, Patrick Peacock decided to go for a walk outside the Gardens. Crossing Museum Street in the middle of the day, he nearly caused a major traffic jam. Cars and buses ground to a halt as he sauntered regally across the road. He stopped at each shop, pecking at their letterboxes and making a right nuisance of himself. Patrick Peacock continued up the road to look at York Minster and marvel at its beauty. Luckily everywhere he went, people and traffic stopped to let him through. "Goodness gracious me!" exclaimed Cyril Squirrel on Patrick's return, "What were you thinking of? You could have died crossing that road. If you want to look at the Minster, just put your head round the gates, and you can see it from there."

"Of course, all the traffic and people stopped for me. Everybody thinks I am wonderful around here and indeed they are right," he proclaimed haughtily. Cyril shook his head. "We have all been very worried about you today, not just the birds and animals, but also the gardeners and the park wardens. Don't be more trouble than you're worth Patrick; otherwise, you will end up eating humble pie!" He was getting a bit exasperated with Patrick's self-importance. What was more worrying was that Patrick was not taking any advice.

Patrick clearly was not happy staying within the Gardens and his bid for freedom did not end there. "I think I am going to take a walk up Bootham," he announced one day. "When I fly onto the Gardens' walls, I can see those wonderful Georgian buildings and the roofs with all those chimney pots, and I think to myself that would be a great adventure."

"I think you've caused enough excitement for one day," Cyril Squirrel murmured with his paws over his eyes as if he could not bear to imagine Patrick walking up another very busy road. "The grass isn't necessarily greener on the other side, you know," he added wisely.

Patrick ignored his friend's advice and the next day, flew over the wall to begin his strut up the street. Cyril could hear the traffic horns honking and brakes squealing as Patrick made his way slowly about the town. This time Patrick spent a couple of days away. Cyril and the whole party of peafowl were worried in case he never returned. Cyril was so relieved to see him back in the Gardens a few days later. "Where on earth have you been?" demanded Cyril. "Don't you realise how frightened we were? We are so glad that you are back safe and sound."

"Oh, I had a tremendous time, Cyril!" Patrick explained in a very loud cocky voice, "I found a hotel and stayed in their gardens for a few days. I was treated like royalty. Everybody loves me. I can pretty much do what I like. Isn't it great!"

"I'll say it again at the risk of being boring, Patrick—pride comes before a fall. Don't say I haven't warned you," and Cyril scampered off into the bushes next to the ruins of St. Mary's Abbey.

A few days later, pandemonium erupted at the library next door and Patrick Peacock's days in the Museum Gardens were numbered. Patrick had decided that he was going to fly onto the roof of the library and frighten all the people silently reading and working there. "Don't be ridiculous!" begged Cyril Squirrel with his paws on his haunches. "Leaving the Gardens is one thing but upsetting the people, your public, is another thing entirely. You and all the peafowl will be banished to a farm outside York if you don't watch your step!" Cyril stood there wringing his paws with fear and trepidation. Patrick ignored him completely.

"What's the point of being your friend if you don't take my advice?" cried Cyril and he sloped off to climb a tree near the Hospitium.

Patrick flew up onto the walls and from there flew onto the roof of the library. He watched through a skylight as all the people quietly went about their business enjoying all the books on every topic under the sun. All at once, he began to peck and scratch at the skylight while crowing and squawking to frighten the people down below. The babies started to cry and an old lady walking through the library had to sit down to recover from the sudden shock. The library staff ran outside angrily to shoo Patrick away off the roof. Eventually, when he became bored of the game, he flew down back into the Gardens and continued as if nothing had happened. Cyril Squirrel ambled past him. "Well you've really gone and done it this time!" Cyril shouted, "Just watch, there will be dire consequences!" He walked off shaking his little grey head in despair.

A few days later, Cyril's words came true. "Now then lad! I'm really sorry to have to tell you that you've come to the end of your road here!" exclaimed the Park Warden to Patrick. "You are more trouble than you're worth! We have decided to send you all to a nearby farm." Patrick's pride had cost him his place in the Gardens. All the squirrels and the pigeons came to the Museum Gardens' gates to wave the party of peafowl off on their journey. They were all very sad to see them go. A big truck pulled up inside the huge gates and all the peafowl were guided into it. They were off on their next adventure into the countryside. Patrick Peacock looked around confused and shocked. How had it come to this?

The party of peafowl arrived at their new home, a farm near Sutton Bank. They all trooped out of the truck into the sunlight and began to scratch around on the farmyard for food. There were a few cows for company and a couple of turtle doves flew around their heads. Gone were all the squirrels and the audience of tourists. All of a sudden Proud Patrick realised, too late, that he really had gone too far. He was forced to admit to himself that he had been wrong to act so selfishly. He would indeed have to eat humble pie. "If only I had taken Cyril's advice and realised that pride really does come before a fall," he cried to the skies, "I could still be enjoying life in the Museum Gardens today!" Proud Patrick Peacock had become Poor Patrick Peacock, and he sloped off with his tail feathers down to the far side of the farmyard to be on his own.

Rosalind Gosling Shocks Her Flock!

Gorgeous Gwendolen Goose lived on the shores of Coniston Water in the Lake District. She spent her days waddling around in the yard next to a small white cottage with a grey slate roof. Gwendolen was the leader of her gaggle of geese, and all the geese and goslings looked up to her for advice and wisdom. She was gorgeous to everyone, helping them with whatever was bothering them: big and small problems, huge or tiny worries. Gwendolen made their world a better place with love, generosity and kindness. That's why they called her Gorgeous Gwendolen Goose! Everyone needed her help at present because they were having real problems with Rosalind Gosling, a tiny baby goose, who was driving them all crazy.

"What are we going to do with her, Gwendolen?" asked her mummy, Gracie Goose, in despair. "We are all so worried about Rosalind. She just keeps telling lies. The first lies were small ones but now they seem to be growing into bigger and bigger lies. Soon no-one will trust or respect her."

"That's strange," murmured Gwendolen, her big blue eyes looking thoughtful. "She knows she should always tell the truth and the rest of us do, so why has she decided to choose to lie? It doesn't make any sense. Don't worry Gracie. We shall all keep an eye on her and try to find out what's going on." Rosalind Gosling was very cute with yellow and brown fluffy feathers, a bright orange bill and big orange webbed feet. She was going to grow into a fine white goose but for now, she ran round the yard getting under everybody's webbed feet honking her very loudest. You could hear her honking right across the yard. "Stop honking so loudly," all the geese would call out to Rosalind. 'We can't hear ourselves think."

"Yes, your honking is too noisy, and you're not saying anything important!" added Lucy Goose.

"Well if you think I'm loud you ought to hear my older sister Gabriella Goose honk," sneered Rosalind. "She has even been down to London and won The Honk Factor on television!"

Lucy Goose looked at Rosalind shocked by that blatant lie and hissed, "If you carry on saying things like that, you will upset everybody." Gabriella Goose stuck her long graceful neck round the corner of the goose shed and looked at her little sister with disdain, "I've never even flown further than Ambleside you silly gosling! How could I get all the way to London, and I've never been on television!" Rosalind strutted off to the corner of the yard to sulk. Later on, her mummy, Gracie, came to have a chat with her.

"You know our honking shouldn't be loud and noisy.

It isn't a competition. We should be honking to be kind and encouraging to each other. If you haven't got anything truthful or kind to honk then don't honk at all." Gracie gave Rosalind a loving peck on the bill but she couldn't help worrying why her daughter was telling lies.

A week later, the geese were contentedly scratching for food near the water's edge. The sky was a diamond blue and the trees, the mountains and the boats were reflected in the steel blue waters of the lake. Suddenly, out of nowhere, Rosalind proclaimed at the top of her voice, "My mummy can fly higher and faster than all the other geese in our yard!"

"That's not true!" replied one of the smaller goslings angrily. "All our parents, geese and ganders, fly in a V-formation whenever they can so that they use each other's updraft. They all work as a team like we all should! Don't you know that Rosalind, you're so stupid!" With her bill in the air, Rosalind waddled off to be on her own. The geese left her on her own but she didn't come back to them and apologise. The whole gaggle wondered why Rosalind was being so annoying, and they were starting to run out of patience. The very next day, Rosalind Gosling announced in the middle of the yard, "My daddy's gone and is never coming back!"

The gaggle of geese looked at her in stunned silence. They were all shocked and upset. Her mummy, Gracie Goose, turned towards her and said, "Don't be silly Rosalind! You're frightening all the little goslings. You know where he is. When we were flying last week, his friend Alexander Gander was hurt and had to fly to the ground. Daddy is staying with him until Alexander feels better. Then he will fly home with him. That's what we always do when one of our flock gets ill. Don't worry, he will be back soon." She put a motherly wing around her daughter and guided her over to Gorgeous Gwendolen Goose, who now took her turn to talk to Rosalind.

"Why did you say that about your Daddy?" Gwendolen said quietly to Rosalind. Rosalind looked at Gwendolen and her mummy, Gracie, and burst into tears. "Nobody listens to me, and everybody hates me," she cried. "We do listen to you, and we all love you. Maybe we just don't tell you often enough," comforted Gwendolen, "There is only one Rosalind Gosling in the world, and you are funny, and helpful and kind, and we are very proud of you except ... when you are telling lies!"

"How do you think we can help you always to tell the truth," asked Gracie. "I don't know, Mummy," sobbed Rosalind, "Some things I don't understand and so I just make them up and sometimes I just want people to listen to me instead of ignoring me."

"That's really interesting Rosalind," said Gwendolen with a smile, "You clearly have a fantastic imagination. Let's put this strength to good use. Why don't you ask us questions about the things you don't understand?" Rosalind nodded in agreement. "...And why don't you tell us all a story every night before we all go to sleep," added Gwendolen, "so that everybody listens to the fantastic ideas you've had throughout the day."

"That sounds like a good plan Gwendolen," Rosalind answered thoughtfully. "I think I also need to listen to others to learn from them and get some good ideas for my stories."

"That is a brilliant idea Rosalind," replied Gwendolen enthusiastically. "If you listen to others respectfully they will do the same to you. If you give love you will receive love, Rosalind. It's how we earn trust and respect. Then you will feel so much better about yourself and the rest of our flock and start to love yourself like we love you." Gracie, Rosalind and Gwendolen all smiled at each other. Rosalind had learned a huge lesson today about how she was going to make better choices and in turn make her world a better, happier place.

Dougal Eagle Flies High!

Dougal Eagle lived on the mountain overlooking Lochranza on the beautiful Isle of Arran in Scotland. He lived there with his mother, Mabel, and his father, Fergal. Each day, he would leave the ledge up high near the mountain's summit to go to the big school in Lamlash.

Dougal was a very clever eagle, using his eagle eyes to learn everything he could about the wonderful world around him.

He really enjoyed flying to school and being with his eagle friends and learning different subjects. He loved learning languages: German with Herr Adler, French with Madame Aigle, Chinese with Mr Ying and English with Mrs Bird. His science, history, geography, music, art, Information Communication Technology and maths teachers praised him to the skies for his hard work and perseverance. However, his favourite subjects were Technology with Mr Aviary and Sport with the Headteacher Mrs Aquiline, who, like her name suggests, had an enormous beak.

Every day, he would leave Lochranza in the early morning light, looking forward to the day ahead at school. He would fly low over the deer in the valley below.

Then he would soar above the sea over the fish, the seals and the dolphins beneath him.

What a fabulous journey he had to school! His favourite days were those where he was studying Technology, building different kinds of nests in every shape and size and situation, and practising sport, learning how to fly quicker and higher, and how to dive like a falling stone to catch his next meal out in the wild.

Mrs Aquiline was particularly proud of his sporting skills and Dougal had represented his school in several flying competitions across the country. He had won lots of medals and cups in his particular speciality, 'Soaring and Gliding.'

One day, Mrs Aquiline called Dougal into her office, which she had decorated like an eagle's nest or eyrie. "I want to discuss your career options with you before you leave us Dougal," she explained to him.

"You have the whole world in front of you, and you can be anything you want to be. I am sure you will be a famous eagle throughout the world if you carry on making the best of every opportunity as you do now. We think you are amazing, and I know your mother, Mabel, and father, Fergal, are fiercely proud of all your efforts."

"I really haven't made up my mind yet what I want to be, Mrs Aquiline," Dougal replied with his feathered brow all furrowed and his brown eagle eyes looking down at the floor.

"Well I think, the best way is for you to go and experience some different kinds of jobs and see which path you would like to follow," reassured Mrs Aquiline kindly.

"Choice is your ultimate luxury Dougal and because you are so good at all your subjects, you can choose whatever you would like to be. Keep your options open because in your lifetime, jobs will change. Some jobs haven't even been invented yet! Imagine that!" she exclaimed. She got up from her desk and started to walk around the eyrie with her wings clasped behind her back, her large beak leading her round the office.

"You could be a legal eagle!" she exclaimed looking Dougal straight in the eye, "a lawyer, making sure all the eagles do things right." Dougal put his head to one side and thought about this and then began to nod his head sagely.

"You could be a medical eagle, a nautical eagle or a musical eagle," she proclaimed, getting into her stride, describing different professions as she imagined Dougal's life stretching out ahead. Dougal, however, was beginning to get a little confused and scratched his head with his wing feathers.

"You could be a theatrical eagle, a political eagle, an

electrical eagle or a mechanical eagle!" she screeched, getting ever more excited with each syllable.

Mrs Aquiline was gearing up for her finest selection of adjectives as she continued, "You could be a pedagogical, pharmaceutical, aeronautical, agricultural, zoological, petrochemical or technological eagle!" She stopped to get her breath as she quietly announced her final two six-syllable professions with pride in her amazing command of the language, "You could be an ecclesiastical eagle or indeed an ornithological eagle." Mrs Aquiline took her seat behind her desk, folded her wings in front of her and closed her eyes, silently pleased with this list of careers that Dougal could follow.

Dougal stood there in her office a little confused by some of the words but keen to confirm exactly what they meant. "Please can I just check what I think you said there?" Dougal wisely clarified without sounding cheeky or stupid. "I could work in law, health, shipping or music, the theatre, politics, construction, education, medicine, aircraft, farming, animals, energy development or digital technology and finally, work for the church or look after birds. Is that the list at the moment?" He looked at her with his eagle eyes shining at all the exciting possibilities.

"You are indeed a very able eagle, Dougal", Mrs Aquiline confirmed with a smile. "Yes, you can choose any of these or others if you wish."

"I love flying out over the sea, Mrs Aquiline," enthused Dougal, "so I think I could start by working on a boat." Mrs Aquiline arranged for Dougal to spend a week on a fishing trawler, working in the crow's nest, on the lookout for any hazards out at sea using his eagle eyes. Unfortunately, it wasn't long before Dougal was back at school in Lamlash, looking decidedly green about the gills. Dougal had suffered from shocking seasickness up there in the crow's nest on the ship, and he realised that a life on the ocean's waves was not for him.

"I love being here at school with you and all my fellow eagles, Mrs Aquiline. What if I start to think about being a teacher?"

"A noble profession, Dougal," pronounced Mrs Aquiline, sniffing emotionally. "You can start on Monday in Junior Eaglet one with Mrs Feather."

Dougal admired Mrs Feather's enthusiasm and skill but at the end of the week, he came to Mrs Aquiline convinced that this career just wasn't for him.

"Mrs Feather has unending amounts of patience, Mrs Aquiline. Even when the eaglets have made such a mess at lunchtime eating their meals and end up squawking at each other in the playground, she never gets angry but helps them to be the best versions of themselves. I know I would never have that much patience."

Dougal reflected again on what career he might follow and asked Mrs Aquiline if he could visit a lawyer to see whether this might be the path for him.

"You'll have to fly over to Kilmarnock to visit the courts there.'

Mrs Aquiline replied, "I have a wonderful colleague Mr Judge who will guide you through the world of law! You'll love it!" And indeed, he did.

As soon as he arrived, he realised that this would be the path for him. He could use all his studies and his skills to help the world become a better place, to encourage eagles to live good law-abiding lives and to make sure that truth and justice prevailed.

He returned to Arran to his parents, Mabel and Fergal, and to Mrs Aquiline and his friends at school with increased confidence in himself.

He was enthusiastic and wanted to work hard and always to be the best version of himself. There was nothing he couldn't do.

"It's an exciting challenge," Dougal explained to his parents as they settled down on the ledge in Lochranza to sleep. "But all the effort is going to be worthwhile if I can help the world become a better place!" And they all drifted off to sleep excited about the future, content with a good day's work and thankful for fun, laughter and love. What more could you ask for?

Samantha and Samuel Seagull Love Fair Play!

Samantha and Samuel Seagull lived near the Liver Buildings at the Pier Head in the Port of Liverpool. They often perched right up high on top of the copper Liver Bird statues. They loved to watch the people walking around the seafront below, the boats sailing up and down the River Mersey and the clouds scudding across the sky.

They also loved their football. Although they were twins, they each supported a different football club. Samantha supported Liverpool, the 'Reds', and wore her red scarf with pride; Samuel supported Everton, the 'Toffees', and was never seen without his beloved blue scarf. They both supported each other though, and would go to every home game together to watch the match.

Everton play at Goodison Park and Liverpool play at Anfield, and both grounds are built on either side of Stanley Park, so it wasn't very far to fly. Samantha and Samuel would perch right on the top of the stadium roof so they could get a bird's eye view looking down on the match below.

"I love everything about football, Samuel! Look how big the stadium is! Look how green the pitch is! It's all so exciting!" Samantha squawked one Saturday afternoon, just before kick-off at Anfield.

"I love football too, our kid!' replied Samuel. "It is indeed the beautiful game, the best game ever!"

"Why do they call football the beautiful game, Samuel?" asked Samantha.

"Football is the most popular game in the world. Anyone can play football, and there are millions of supporters just like us," he chirruped.

"Oh, I hope we win today!" interrupted Samantha nervously. She was always jittery before a match. "Let's have plenty of goals! I hate games without goals!" she continued.

"Yes!" chirped Samuel as the referee blew the whistle at the start of the match, "Fair play to both teams as well to make sure the beautiful game stays beautiful!"

"Yes, indeed," replied Samantha wisely, "Fair play in all sports and pastimes too: football, cricket, rugby, horse-riding, karate and chess—the list is endless."

Just then the Liverpool supporters, with one voice, sang their anthem "You'll never walk alone" all with passion and pride. The noise was deafening.

"I always cry when they sing our song," cooed Samantha,

and a little tear dripped down her white-feathered face. "The words to this song are so lovely," she cried and she joined in the final chorus along with the capacity crowd: 'Walk on, walk on, with hope in your heart, and you'll never walk alone. You'll ne-ver walk a-lo-o-one."

"You're so soppy Samantha," squawked Samuel, and he launched, with gusto, into a loud rendition of: 'It's a grand old team to play for! It's a grand old team to support! And if you know your history, it's enough to make your heart go bo-o-o-om!' "Everton's song is fantastic! Each football team has its own special anthem, songs and chants which tell the history of each club—it's so clever! We are all so proud of our teams!" Then, they both turned their attention to the football match below them to enjoy the afternoon's entertainment.

Samantha and Samuel not only liked watching football, they loved playing football too. In the early morning light, when the tide was out, before any people were around, Samuel and Samantha would go to play football with their seagull friends on Crosby Beach. Other spectator birds would perch on the railings on the seafront looking down onto the sand as the two seagull teams played their games.

The seagulls used the Iron Men statues as goal posts and a shell as the ball. They could scuffle along the sand with their webbed feet kicking the shell but also they could pick the shell up in their beaks and fly towards the goal. The seagulls tried various acrobatic movements to get the shell over the goal line. The spectators thought it was very funny to see the seagulls dodging and weaving between each other almost like they were dancing to music.

One of their cormorant bird friends was referee, and you could clearly see his black feathers in the midst of all the white-feathered seagulls. At the beginning of every match he would announce: "Remember friends, we want fair play throughout the match—stick to the rules, respect each other and me, the referee, and we will have a fabulous match." Even though it was a friendly match, both teams wanted to win, yet they still wanted the game to be fair and good-natured.

One warm morning, as the light across the beach became brighter, Samantha and Samuel arrived to play football. The two captains touched wings before the start, and the game began.

There were hardly any cross words or angry tackles and the cormorant was pleased with the high standard of fair play by all the members of both teams. Samantha and Samuel's team were just about to score a goal when the shell bounced up and hit Samuel on the wing. "Wing-ball!" the opposing team shouted with passion as this meant that it was their free kick. Samuel turned round to the referee and agreed, "Yes, the shell did hit my wing. The free kick belongs to the other team." Both teams flapped their wings in agreement and shouted "Good fair play, Samuel! Well done!" and the game continued. Sometimes Samantha's and Samuel's team would win and other times the visiting team would win but they always congratulated each other on their skill and sportsmanship. "Well done both teams— a fantastic game of football! Fair play all round!" crowed the cormorant at the end of yet another enjoyable game. Then the sun rose, and people started arriving at the beach to enjoy the early morning.

The football match was over for another day, and all the seagulls flew off to scavenge for a well-earned breakfast.

The sportsmanship and fair play of the seagulls' football was tweeted to Officer Heather Feather, who was in charge of the bird police along the coast. "Congratulations on being honest and respectful to everyone on the pitch. It's always great to hear about fair play in our great city," she announced. She arranged for Samantha and Samuel and all the seagull football players to receive a special badge of honour. She presented the badges to them all on the balcony of Liverpool Town Hall, a building set back from the Pier Head.

Samantha's and Samuel's parents, Sandra and Sandy Seagull, watched with pride. The audience of bird friends and relations took their places on every possible part of the Town Hall: the dome on the roof with the statue of Minerva the ancient goddess of wisdom; the railings all around the Town Hall decorated with elephants and pineapples and the balcony itself where the Royal Family, The Beatles and both football teams have appeared. The birds whistled and crowed their appreciation.

Samantha and Samuel were very proud to be part of teams committed to fair play and enjoyment. They would always continue to watch and play football in their great city of Liverpool. At the end of every day, they would fly off to roost on top of the Liver Birds at the Pier Head and watch the brilliant sunsets while thinking about the beautiful game!

45

Oliver Owl

Is a

Silly Billy!

Oliver Owl had come to visit his wise grandma Prudence. She lived in the wonderful city of Sheffield in South Yorkshire. He loved coming to visit her as she was good company and always looked on the bright side of life. She was a perky, quirky lady with a huge, hopeful heart. Everyone called her Sunny Funny Owl because of her remarkably unique sense of humour and her big, brown, twinkly smiley eyes—and... she made the best Yorkshire Puddings Oliver had ever tasted!

Oliver arrived that evening with a scowl across his beautiful heart-shaped face.

"You look an itsy-bitsy bit angry to me Oliver!" hooted Sunny Funny Owl, "What's up?"

"Oh, Sunny Funny, I have been such a Silly Billy when I want to be a Clever Trevor!" shrieked Oliver with his wings all hunched up. "My friends from Owlets Primary School in Owlerton invited me to a football match. I was so pleased to be asked out by my flock that I forgot to plan for the trip. It was snowy, blowy but I didn't wear my football hat and scarf and my big thick coat so I was as cold as ice by the end of the match. I wasn't too sure of the rules so I didn't know when to clap or shout or cheer. I didn't realise the fans sang songs too. I was silent and frozen for the whole game. It was no fun at all. To make matters even worse, my friends had all taken pocket money for chips with gravy at half time, and you know how much I love chips with gravy, so I was particularly peckish too," he simpered, feeling very sorry for himself.

Sunny Funny Owl looked at Oliver affectionately with her smiley eyes and squawked, "Well, a wise owl learns from mistakes and thinks about how to make the next trip out even better. So chin up, think ahead next time, and you will be okey-dokey," and she gave him a huge hug to make him feel better.

A few weeks later, Oliver Owl came to stay with Sunny Funny Owl again. He landed with a dull thud on the branch of the tree.

"Jeepers Creepers!" exclaimed Sunny Funny Owl, "You look as if you have been mobbed by a murder of crows, Oliver! What's up?"

"Oh Sunny Funny, I have been such a Silly Billy!" Oliver hissed in anger. After the football fiasco, I was so pleased to be asked out to the cinema with my flock that I thought about what I had learnt, and I went to the cinema so happy-flappy! But after only a few minutes, the cinema staff asked me to leave!"

"Deary meary!" gasped Sunny Funny Owl, "What a to-do! What happened?"

"Well I went to the cinema all wrapped up in my warm coat, football hat and scarf, but I was so hot that I had to take them all off one by one and everybody behind me complained. Then I started to clap and shout and cheer after every couple of sentences and then..." Oliver Owl looked down in embarrassment, "...the crunch came, literally, when I opened a family-size bag of crisps, and everybody around me complained that they couldn't hear the film. So I had to leave the cinema." A big tear rolled down Oliver's white-feathered face and he whispered, "I'll never be asked out again."

Sunny Funny Owl smiled at her grandson and announced, "We need a better plan than this! If you fail to plan, you plan to fail! Next time, ask a friend the sticky tricky question, 'What do I have to think about for my next trip?' Then remember what you have learnt from your cinema setback. You need to be a teeny-weeny bit wiser Oliver when planning ahead and consider there's no such thing as a stupid question! You should have worn what you do at home, taken wine gums with you to eat as they make no noise and above all kept quiet!" Sunny Funny Owl put the tip of her wing to her beak. Oliver smiled knowing he had a plan for the next trip out, if his friends ever asked him out again. "It's easy-peasy lemon-squeezy planning ahead!" added Sunny Funny Owl.

On a hot evening in May, Oliver paid his next visit to Sunny Funny Owl. She could see him flying towards her, his feathers drooping and bedraggled.

"Golly gosh!" screeched Sunny Funny Owl "You look as if you have swallowed a poisoned mouse! What's up?"

"My friends asked me out to a picnic by the river. So I asked my friend Orlando Owl what I should think about for this trip." Sunny Funny Owl smiled and nodded. "Clever Trevor!" she said and winked. "But ... I forgot to listen to the answer!" Oliver shook his head from side to side. "So I turned up in my T-shirt with a packet of wine gums and sat quietly by the riverbank for the whole afternoon. My friends all had a tremendous time in their swimming kit jumping in and out of the river, eating loads of sandwiches and drinking gallons of fizzy pop!" Oliver's voice faltered, and he burst into a flood of owly tears. His boo-hoots continued until Sunny Funny Owl offered him a swanky hanky to dry his tears. He stopped sobbing and sniffed softly. "Next time I will definitely ask the question, AND listen to the answer!" he pronounced and his voice grew stronger as he got to the end of the sentence. Sunny Funny Owl gave him a grandmotherly hug and exclaimed, "I love your yearning for learning Oliver. Put this hoo-ha behind you and tell me, what questions do you think you need to ask next time?"

Oliver Owl burst into a fresh bout of blubbering and bawling. Then he stopped crying, slowly took a deep breath, reflected on the shocking shambles he had got himself into and replied calmly, "I need to ask what's going to happen, what I should wear and what to bring with me." His smiley eyes met Sunny Funny Owl's smiley eyes, and he chuckled, "And...I need to listen to the answers."

"You are growing into a very wise owl Oliver," squawked Sunny Funny Owl. "I am very proud of your plucky-lucky stick-ability. Don't shilly-shally and don't give up!" and she squeezed his wing affectionately.

On a hot July evening, a month later, Oliver flew onto Sunny Funny Owl's favourite tree with his bushy tail feathers sticking out with pride. His beautiful white-feathered chest was puffed up with delight and his twinkly brown eyes shone with joy and happiness. "Guess what happened today, Sunny Funny?" he screeched with glee.

"You look a happy chappy Oliver! Tell me what happened?" replied Sunny Funny Owl.

"Well, I was invited to a party with a barbecue by my friend Ophelia Owl. So I remembered the picnic pickle and asked, 'What's going to happen at the party and barbecue? What should I wear?' and 'What should I bring with me?' I could tell that Ophelia was very impressed that I was making such an effort to make her party and barbecue such a success. She described the barbecue in the garden and the party in the house. So I took a jumper to keep me warm in the cool chill of the evening. I took some sausages to eat and a bottle of fizzy pop to share with the whole parliament of my owl friends from Owlets Primary School. We strutted our stuff on the dance floor and had a perfect party with no dismal disasters. I had a tremendous time!"

"Super-duper Oliver—now that's worth a celebration!"

replied Sunny Funny Owl "You need a treat for making good wise choices! Have you got an appetite for some Yorkshire Puddings with chips and gravy after your barbecue?" laughed Sunny Funny Owl.

"Always!" squawked Oliver with a proud self-satisfied grin.

"A perfect end to a perfect day," remarked Sunny Funny Owl. "Remember, ask the right questions and listen to the answers, it's easy-peasy lemon-squeezy!"

Welcome

Summer Swift!

Summer Swift flew through the night with the rest of her flock towards the capital city of the United Kingdom, London. She loved this flight in late April away from the heat of Africa. She flew beneath the brilliant white diamond stars shining against the backdrop of dark blue velvet skies. London in the summertime—she couldn't wait!

Summer Swift arrived as the dawn broke, and she marvelled at the River Thames snaking its way through the city. She came to rest on her usual nesting site at London Zoo; this is where she would lay her eggs and watch her little brood come to life. She flew over Robert Street. Her old friend Robert Redbreast, who was hopping around a little garden, heard her loud shrill screaming call before he saw her. He then recognised her dark brown crescent-shaped wings, and her deeply forked tail silhouetted against the morning sky. "Hey Summer!" he shouted up towards the rooftops. "Is that you?"

"It is indeed!" screamed Summer, as she very briefly came to rest clinging to the side of a house with her hawk-like toes. "Welcome Summer!" squawked Robert happily, "and welcome to summertime now that you have all arrived back from Africa! All my friends Roger, Rosie, Rhiannon,

Ronan and, of course, our famous friend Robin will all be pleased to see you as you herald the arrival of the new season! We are always so delighted to welcome you and all our other visitors into the United Kingdom."

Robert was so excited at the prospect of yet another fabulous day and the start of the wonderful season of summer. As Summer and the rest of her flock arrived, he imagined the long lazy, hazy days of cricket, tennis and boating on the Thames with everybody eating bowls of strawberries and cream and cucumber sandwiches. He looked up into the sky as Summer set off again wheeling and dashing towards London Zoo and Regent's Park. "We are so lucky to have visitors from far and wide in this great city adding colour, variety and a different view of the world," Robert Redbreast thought to himself, "I shall go and visit all my Redbreast friends and tell them the good news that the Swifts are back in town!" Robert Redbreast set off with enthusiasm. As usual, he sang 'Carpe Diem', the Latin phrase for 'Seize the Day' over and over again, as he flew from garden to garden.

Meanwhile, Summer laid her eggs in the nest in London Zoo. She would have about six weeks now to visit all her favourite sights in London while her little family grew.

Each day, she chose a famous place to visit: sometimes it would be a building and other times it would be one of the many parks throughout the city. She caught flies and insects in her large broad mouth to feed on as her tiny beautiful body glided from place to place.

Summer flew to the Royal Albert Hall near Kensington Gardens. She loved to see its circular shape rising in the distance before her. She flew over its glazed iron roof and took a couple of turns round the mosaic frieze, the decorated band which decorates the top of the building. She looked at all the pictures on the frieze depicting people from different countries across the world who have contributed to arts and science. She enjoyed hearing the music drifting upwards from the building. The notes from the famous organ reverberated loudly around the Hall. Every time she visited the Hall, musicians travelling from all four corners of the globe would be playing a different genre of music. The Royal Albert Hall was a truly amazing place!

Every year, Summer would make sure she called in to see the Queen at Buckingham Palace. She waited until the Royal Standard flag was flying above the building showing that the Queen was at home. She flew over the Palace taking time to linger over the beautiful gardens. She loved to watch the soldiers 'changing the guard'. The regimental band played as the soldiers marched in and out of the Palace dressed in their striking scarlet tunics, white belts, black trousers, boots and tall bearskin hats. Summer enjoyed watching the 'Changing of the Guard' with the crowd of people outside the Palace. They were from all parts of the world: not only those who lived in the United Kingdom but also those who were visiting, like her, chattering away in a myriad of different languages. She flew in and out of the famous balcony just in case she caught a glimpse of the Queen or any member of the Royal Family walking around inside the Palace. It was always so exciting!

Sometimes she flew to Bushy Park or Richmond Park just to catch a glimpse of the many deer roaming around. She was fascinated that any animal could live with antlers sticking out of their heads. Their shape was in stark contrast to her tiny, sleek body. She flew past the noisy green ring-necked parakeets who, like her, had come from far away but had settled in this beautiful city and were thriving in the many parks around the capital. "It takes all sorts to make a world!" she thought to herself, "And variety is the spice of life!"

Summer loved to fly to the Houses of Parliament and would take a few moments to cling onto the sides of the beautiful Elizabeth Tower as the Big Ben Bell chimed. She watched the red double-decker buses and the black taxis go roaring past. She then flew off swooping and wheeling around the roofs of the government buildings on the banks of the Thames.

Summer always made sure she flew to Tower Bridge. From there she could easily dart over the Tower of London avoiding the huge black ravens who live there. Then she would cross the river to fly around the Shard, the **95**-storey skyscraper, in which she could see her reflection and the reflection of the intriguing skyline around her. Summer liked to look at the old and the new buildings living next to each other, complementing each other's style, shape and size. "It's just like everywhere on this lovely planet: differences living in harmony with each other," she reflected.

Every night, she continued to fly around the city with her flock. From Wanstead to Pinner, she soared catching more and more insects. She would then take them all home, packed tightly in her throat, to feed her little fledgling family, who grew stronger every day.

Soon it was late August. Summer Swift's little family had already flown the nest, and it was time to migrate again back to Africa. Summer flew over Robert Redbreast's little garden to say her goodbyes. She had had another fantastic summer season in London enjoying every aspect of this vibrant city. "We wish you well Summer!" exclaimed Robert Redbreast, "Until you come back again. Remember, we always welcome everyone from all around the world. We also appreciate you when you are here as we know we won't have your marvellous company for long. We cherish the days you spend here with us."

"I've had a fantastic time," screamed Summer shrilly, "I always feel welcome and at home in London. I'll be back next year, without fail!" Without further ado, she soared into the evening sky with the rest of her flock, fit for the long journey south and already relishing the idea of her return journey back to London next year.

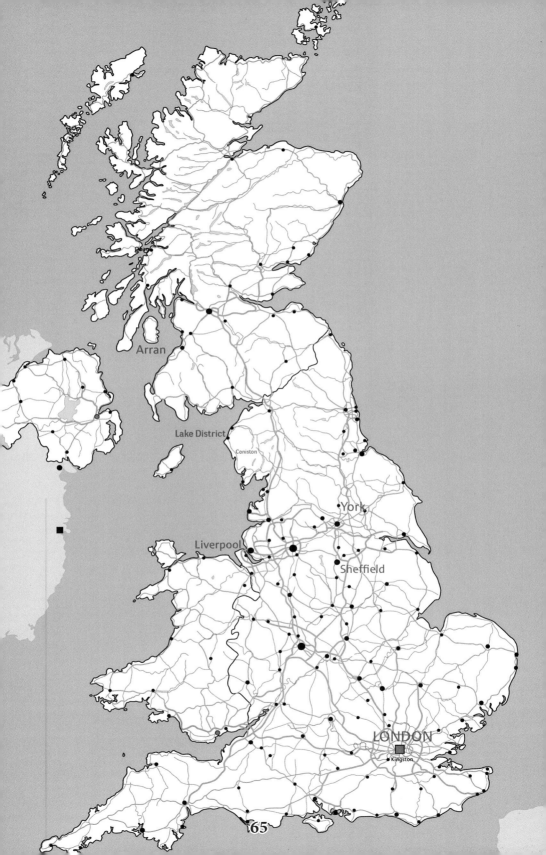

Arran

Lake District

Coniston

York

Liverpool

Sheffield

LONDON

Kingston